W9-AGD-525

This book belongs to

_____

_____

_____

Age _____

© 1992 Grandreams Limited.
This edition published in 1995.

Adapted from the originals by Anne McKie.
Illustrated by Ken McKie.

Published by
GRANDREAMS LIMITED
Jadwin House, 205/211 Kentish Town Road, London, NW5

Printed in Czech Republic.

FN1

Fairy Tales in this book

Red Riding Hood

Aladdin

Sleeping Beauty

The Gingerbread Man

**plus a selection of your favourite
Nursery Rhymes**

Red Riding Hood

Once upon a time there was a little girl who lived with her parents in a cottage on the edge of a forest. Her father was a woodcutter. He worked all day long in the forest, chopping down trees with his huge axe.

Right in the middle of the forest was another cottage. It belonged to the little girl's Grandmother.

The kind old lady loved her grand-daughter very much, so one day she decided to make her a present. It was a red cloak with a red hood to match.

The cloak looked so nice that the little girl wore it all the time. And that is why everybody called her Red Riding Hood.

But one day the Grandmother felt ill, so Red Riding Hood's mother baked her a cake and made her some fresh butter — just to make her feel better.

"Red Riding Hood," called her mother. "Take this cake and butter to Grandmother's cottage, a visit from you will cheer her up!"

So Red Riding Hood picked up the basket, waved goodbye to her mother and went off down the path.

She hadn't gone very far when she met a wolf. He trotted up pretending to be friendly. "Good morning, Red Riding Hood. What have you got in your basket today?"

"I have some fresh butter and cake," replied the little girl. "They are for my Grandmother, who lives in the middle of the forest. She is ill and needs cheering up."

The wolf licked his lips. "How I would love to gobble this tasty little girl up. But if I am clever, I can eat her Grandmother as well," he sniggered. "Red Riding Hood," said the wolf slyly. "We will both go to visit your Grandmother and cheer her up. I'll race you there!"

Then the clever wolf said to Red Riding Hood, "You follow this path and I will find another one. Then we'll see who reaches Grandmother's cottage first."

No sooner was Red Riding Hood out of sight than the wolf ran off at top speed.

As for Red Riding Hood, she wandered slowly along the path picking flowers and wild strawberries for her Grandmother. She had forgotten all about the race.

That wicked wolf knew every secret path and short cut in the forest. He ran so fast, the animals and birds never even noticed him.

Quietly he crept round a clearing in the trees where the woodcutter was chopping wood. On and on he raced until he came to the middle of the forest.

The wolf reached Grandmother's cottage in next to no time. He ran up the path and knocked on the door.

"Who is that?" cried Grandmother from her bed. "It is Red Riding Hood," replied the wolf in his softest voice. "Lift the latch and come right in," the old lady called, "the door isn't locked, my dear."

The wolf bounded in and swallowed poor Grandmother in one bite!

"That was delicious," sighed the wicked wolf, smacking his lips. "Now for Red Riding Hood!"

The wolf looked round the bedroom. He found one of Grandmother's spare nightdresses and her nightcap, so he put them on as fast as he could.

Then he noticed a spare pair of Grandmother's glasses, so he stuck them on the end of his nose. Then the wolf jumped into bed and waited for Red Riding Hood.

At last the little girl reached the cottage door and tapped very gently. "Who is it?" asked the wolf (trying to sound like Grandmother).

"It's Red Riding Hood and I've brought you some cake and fresh butter."

The wolf grinned. "Lift the latch and walk right in," he croaked.

So Red Riding Hood opened the door and came inside. "You sound very strange," called Red Riding Hood up the stairs to her Grandmother. "I have a cold, my dear!" the wolf replied. "Come upstairs so that I can see you."

Little Red Riding Hood was rather shocked when she saw her Grandmother. She looked so different.

"Why, Grandmother, what strong arms you have!" said the little girl.

"All the better to hug you with!" replied the wolf.

"Why, Grandmother, what big ears you have!" said Red Riding Hood.

"All the better to hear you with!" the wolf cried.

"Why, Grandmother, what big eyes you have!" said Red Riding Hood staring at him.

"All the better to see you with!" the wolf grinned.

"Why, Grandmother, what big teeth you have!" gasped Red Riding Hood.

"All the better to EAT you with!" snarled the wolf. And he threw back the bed clothes and leapt out of bed.

Poor Red Riding Hood screamed at the top of her voice, as the wolf tried to grab her and gobble her up. She escaped from the bedroom and dashed down the stairs — the hungry wolf close behind!

Now, Red Riding Hood's father was chopping wood nearby and he heard the little girl's screams.

The woodcutter grabbed his huge axe and ran towards the cottage. he saw the wolf chasing Red Riding Hood and guessed what had happened. The brave woodcutter raised his axe and chopped the wolf in two with one blow. The wolf fell dead, and Red Riding Hood was saved.

The frightened little girl ran to her father and kissed and hugged him.

But what a surprise they got when they turned round . . . there stood Grandmother safe and sound! Because the woodcutter had chopped the wolf in two, Grandmother was able to climb out quite unharmed.

So all three went back inside the cottage. They unpacked the basket Red Riding Hood had brought and had some cake spread with fresh butter.

Little Red Riding Hood never again went walking in the forest alone. And Grandmother took great care to lock her cottage door.

Polly put the kettle on,
Polly put the kettle on,
Polly put the kettle on,
  We'll all have tea.

Sukey take it off again,
Sukey take it off again,
Sukey take it off again,
  They've all gone away.

It's raining, it's pouring,
The old man's snoring;
He got into bed
And bumped his head
And couldn't get up in the morning.

Old Mother Goose,
When she wanted to wander,
Would ride through the air
On a very fine gander.

Mother Goose had a house,
'Twas built in a wood,
Where an owl at the door
For sentinel stood.

Hickory, dickory, dock,
     The mouse ran up the clock.
The clock struck one,
     The mouse ran down,
Hickory, dickory, dock.

Jack be nimble,
     Jack be quick,
Jack jump over
     The candlestick.

As I was going to St Ives,
I met a man with seven wives;

Each wife had seven sacks,

Each sack had seven cats,

Each cat had seven kits:

Kits, cats, sacks and wives
How many were going to St Ives?

Little Blue Ben, who lives in the glen,
Keeps a blue cat and one blue hen,
Which lays of blue eggs a score and ten;
Where shall I find the little Blue Ben?

Yankee Doodle came to town,
Riding on a pony,
He stuck a feather in his cap
And called it macaroni.

Bobby Shaftoe's gone to sea,
　　Silver buckles on his knee;
He'll come back and marry me,
　　Bonny Bobby Shaftoe.

Bobby Shaftoe's bright and fair,
　　Combing down his yellow hair,
He's my love for evermore,
　　Bonny Bobby Shaftoe.

This little pig went to market;

This little pig stayed at home;

This little pig had roast beef;

This little pig had none;
And this little pig cried, Wee-wee-wee!
   All the way home.

JANUARY 31 FEBRUARY 28 MARCH 31 APRIL 30 MAY 31 JUNE 30 JULY 31

AUGUST 31 SEPTEMBER 30 OCTOBER 31 NOVEMBER 30 DECEMBER 31

Thirty days hath September,
April, June and November;
All the rest have thirty-one.
Excepting February alone,
And that has twenty-eight days clear
And twenty-nine in each leap year.

Rub-a-dub-dub,
Three men in a tub,
And how do you think they got there?
The butcher, the baker,
The candlestick-maker,
They all jumped out of a rotten potato.
'Twas enough to make a fish stare.

Humpty Dumpty sat on a wall,
Humpty Dumpty had a great fall;
All the King's horses,
And all the King's men,
Couldn't put Humpty together again.

A diller, a dollar,
A ten o'clock scholar,
What makes you come so soon?
You used to come at ten o'clock,
But now you come at noon.

Pat-a-cake, pat-a-cake, baker's man,
Bake me a cake as fast as you can;
Pat it and prick it, and mark it with B,
Put it in the oven for Baby and me.

Aladdin

This strange story happened in a city in far-off China many years ago. It is a tale of a magic lamp, a magic ring, an evil magician and many more amazing things. But most of all, it is a story about a boy called Aladdin.

Aladdin was the son of a poor widow. Although his mother worked hard to earn a little money, her son did nothing to help her. He spent all his time with his friends, day-dreaming of becoming a rich man.

One day, as Aladdin was just lazing around, a stranger came up to him. "I am your uncle from Africa," said the man. "Go home and tell your mother I am coming to visit her."

For once Aladdin did as he was told.

The poor widow used all the money she had to buy food for the stranger's supper. After he had eaten, the man promised to make them both rich. Aladdin was delighted — but his mother was not so sure.

"All I ask," said the stranger, "is that Aladdin do one small task for me tomorrow in return."

Now as you may have guessed, the stranger was not Aladdin's uncle at all. He was really a powerful magician in disguise. He was not out to help Aladdin — but trick him.

Very early next morning,
Aladdin and the magician left
the city. By the time it was light
they had reached the
mountains. As they climbed up
and up, the path grew narrower
with steep rocks on each side.
At long last they stopped. They
could go no further for a huge
boulder blocked their path.

Aladdin sat down to rest,
but not for long! The magician
pointed a long finger at the
boulder and shouted,
''Abracadabra''. A noise like
thunder echoed round the
mountains, the boulder
vanished, and the rock behind
cracked in two.

The magician grabbed hold of Aladdin. "Go through that crack in the rock, because I am too big. You will find some steps which lead to a cave, in the cave you will see an old lamp. Bring it to me straight away."

Poor Aladdin tried to run away, but the evil magician held him too tightly.

"If you are such a coward," bellowed the magician, "take my magic ring." And with that he pushed Aladdin through the crack in the rock, and the poor boy fell down the steps and into the cave.

When Aladdin picked himself up, he could hardly believe his eyes. The cave was full of gold and jewels. Aladdin gasped. He picked up a few and stuffed them in his pocket to take back to his mother.

Outside the cave the magician began to shout, ''Bring me my lamp at once!'' But Aladdin was too busy to hear him.

Because Aladdin did not obey him at once, the magician flew into a terrible rage. He shouted the magic word ''Abracadabra'' and the crack in the rock closed and Aladdin was trapped.

The poor boy buried his head in his hands in despair. Now quite by chance he rubbed the magic ring on his finger. Immediately the cave was filled with a loud swishing noise, and an enormous genie appeared. "I'm the Genie of the Ring, O Master! Speak, and I obey!"

"Take me home," gasped Aladdin.

"Your wish is my command," answered the genie. "But first, O Master, take this old lamp. Inside is a genie more powerful than me, and you will become his master."

A great roaring sound filled the air, and Aladdin found himself being carried back home by a genie twice as large as the first one.

Aladdin's mother screamed with fright, until he told her of his adventures and the wonderful lamp.

At last Aladdin's dream had come true and they were no longer poor. He soon became the richest man in the land, thanks to the Genie of the Lamp. The Emperor became his friend and invited him to his court.

One day Aladdin met the Emperor's daughter, and he fell in love with her at once. Aladdin dare not ask the Emperor if he could marry the Princess. So he rubbed the lamp and asked the genie to fill the whole of the Emperor's garden with treasure.

Then the Emperor gladly gave his consent. Aladdin rubbed his lamp again, and a beautiful new palace appeared for Aladdin and the Princess to live in.

Far away in Africa, the evil magician heard about Aladdin's palace. He guessed at once that Aladdin had the lamp.

Straight away he travelled to China. He disguised himself as an old lamp-seller and waited by the gates of Aladdin's palace. ''New lamps for old,'' he cried loudly. He didn't have to wait long before a servant brought out all the old lamps from the palace.

The evil magician saw his lamp and grabbed it with glee. He ordered the genie to take him, the palace and the Princess back to his home in Africa.

When Aladdin returned home he could find no trace of his Princess or his palace.

As he sat wondering what to do, quite by accident he rubbed the magic ring. At once the genie appeared. "Take me to my Princess, O Genie of the Ring!" Aladdin begged.

Before he could even blink, he found himself standing outside her bedroom window. The Princess was overjoyed to see Aladdin. "I know where the lamp is," she whispered. "The magician keeps it tied to his belt night and day."

Quickly Aladdin told her his plan.

"Take this sleeping powder and mix it in his wine. You must steal the lamp as soon as he falls asleep!"

Late that night the Princess dropped the powder into the Magician's glass, although she was very frightened. He fell asleep at once and she carefully untied the lamp.

Aladdin jumped out from his hiding place and grabbed the lamp. One rub and the genie appeared. "Take us all home!" Aladdin cried.

The genie's magic was so powerful, he was able to whisk the palace, the Princess, Aladdin and all the servants back home to China.

"Drop that evil magician into the sea on the way home!" ordered Aladdin.

The Emperor and Aladdin's mother were waiting to welcome them all back home. At last their adventures were over.

As for the lamp, Aladdin made sure it was kept in a very safe place — and never given away again.

Three little kittens
They lost their mittens,
　　And they began to cry,
Oh, Mother dear,
We sadly fear
Our mittens we have lost.
What! Lost your mittens,
You naughty kittens!
Then you shall have no pie.
　　Mee-ow, mee-ow, mee-ow.
No, you shall have no pie.

The three little kittens
They found their mittens,
　　And they began to cry,
Oh, Mother dear,
See here, see here,
Our mittens we have found.
Put on your mittens,
You silly kittens,
And you shall have some pie.
　　Purr-r, purr-r, purr-r,
Oh, let us have some pie.

The three little kittens
Put on their mittens,
    And soon ate up the pie;
Oh, Mother dear,
We greatly fear
Our mittens we have soiled.
What! Soiled your mittens,
You naughty kittens!
Then they began to sigh,
    Mee-ow, mee-ow, mee-ow,
Then they began to sigh.

The three little kittens
They washed their mittens,
    And hung them out to dry;
Oh, Mother dear,
Do you not hear,
Our mittens we have washed.
What! Washed your mittens,
You good little kittens,
But I smell a rat close by.
    Mee-ow, mee-ow, mee-ow,
We smell a rat close by.

The Man in the moon came tumbling down,
To ask his way to Norwich.
He went by the south and burnt his mouth,
By eating cold plum-porridge.

Diddle, diddle, dumpling, my son John,
Went to bed with his trousers on;
One shoe off, and one shoe on,
Diddle, diddle, dumpling, my son John.

One misty, moisty morning,
  When cloudy was the weather,
There I met an old man
  Clothed all in leather.

I took him by the hand,
  And told him very plain,
'How do you do? How do you do?
  And how do you do again?'

Little Tommy Tittlemouse
Lived in a little house;
He caught fishes
In other men's ditches.

PRIVATE
NO FISHING

Sing a song of sixpence,
A pocket full of rye;
Four-and-twenty blackbirds,
Baked in a pie.

When the pie was opened,
The birds began to sing;
Was not that a dainty dish,
To set before the king?

The king was in his counting-house,
Counting out his money;
The queen was in the parlour
Eating bread and honey.

The maid was in the garden,
Hanging out the clothes,
When down came a blackbird
And pecked off her nose.

Little Boy Blue,
Come blow your horn.
The sheep's in the meadow,
The cow's in the corn.
Where is the boy
Who looks after the sheep?
He's under a haystack
Fast asleep.
Will you wake him?
No, not I,
For if I do,
He's sure to cry.

Pease porridge hot,
Pease porridge cold,
Pease porridge in the pot,
    Nine days old.

Some like it hot,   Some like it cold,   Some like it in the pot,
                                                Nine days old.

Curly Locks, Curly Locks,
Wilt thou be mine?
Thou shalt not wash dishes,
Nor yet feed the swine;

But sit on a cushion,
And sew a fine seam
And feed upon strawberries,
Sugar and cream.

SLEEPING BEAUTY

A long time ago in a kingdom far away, a baby Princess was born. The King and Queen were so happy and proud of their little daughter, they invited the most important fairies in the land to come to her christening.

The invitations were sent out and the fairies set off for the palace.

When the christening was over all the fairies crowded round the baby's cradle, the time had come for them to give the Princess her gifts.

The first fairy gave her beauty, the second gave her goodness, the third fairy said she would be charming, the fourth promised she would be clever, the fifth fairy gave her grace and the sixth fairy said she would always be happy.

All of a sudden, the door to the banqueting hall burst open. Standing there was the ugliest most evil-looking fairy you can imagine!

''Why was I not invited?'' she screamed.

The evil fairy shook with anger as she went up to the cradle. The King and Queen trembled as she pointed at the baby Princess.

''Before she is sixteen, the Princess will prick her finger on a spindle and die!'' And with a terrible cackle of laughter, she vanished.

Everyone was shocked by the wicked fairy's spell, and the poor Queen began to cry.

Just at that moment the smallest fairy stepped from behind a pillar where she had been hiding.

''I have not yet given the Princess my gift,'' she said in a kind voice. ''The Princess will not die — but fall asleep for one hundred years. Then a young Prince will come and wake her with a kiss, and the evil spell will be broken.''

That very day the King sent out messengers all over the land.

All the spindles and the spinning wheels were smashed or burned. He made a very strict law that no-one should ever use a spindle again. This way the King hoped to save his dear Princess from the fairy's evil spell.

Sixteen years past. The Princess grew up beautiful, good, charming and happy, in fact she grew up with all the gifts the fairies had promised.

One day she was gazing up at the palace, when she noticed an open window at the very top of the highest tower.

"I wonder if anyone lives up there?" said the Princess. "I think I'll climb right up to the top and see."

Now the palace was a wonderful place to explore, because it was so big and rambling. So the Princess climbed up the winding staircase until she found herself in front of a small door. Gently she pushed it open.

There, in a tiny attic room, sat a little old lady spinning. (She had never heard the King's very strict law about spindles — as she never left her attic room.) "What are you doing?" asked the Princess, very interested.

"Just spinning wool, my dear!" smiled the old lady.

"May I try?" asked the Princess, and she reached out for the spindle. As she touched the sharp point, it pricked her finger.

The evil fairy's spell had worked. At once the Princess fell to the floor in a deep sleep.

When the King and Queen were told what had happened, and when they saw the Princess asleep, they knew the evil spell had come true. Their beloved daughter would sleep for a hundred years.

The servants carried the Princess from the attic room and laid her on a beautiful velvet-covered bed.

Now the good fairy (who promised the Princess would not die) came at once to the Palace. Without a word she touched everybody with her wand.

She touched the cooks in the kitchen, and the servants who waited at the Palace banqueting table.

She touched the guards and the footmen, the pages and the maids.

Her magic wand even sent the Princess's little dog to sleep.

A strange silence fell over everything. Gently, her wand touched the King and Queen before she flew away from the Palace.

The good fairy waved her wand for the last time
and a thick forest sprang up around the Palace.
Tangled briar and thorns crept over the paths and up
the walls. This way no-one could cut through the
undergrowth or visit the sleeping Palace, until one
hundred years had gone by.

As time passed people forgot all about the Palace and the sleeping Princess.

One day a handsome Prince was out hunting nearby. He happened to look up and saw the very tops of the Palace towers peeping above the trees.

From out of nowhere the good fairy appeared! She told him of the Princess and the evil spell that only a handsome Prince like him could break.

At once the Prince drew his sword and began to cut a path through the thick brambles.

Very soon he reached the
Palace. He passed snoring
guards and sleeping ladies and
gentlemen.

The Palace cat was snoozing
peacefully on a cushion.

There were even a couple of
mice fast asleep under the table
in the banqueting hall.

They had all been asleep for
one hundred years.

Suddenly, the Prince looked up and saw the beautiful Princess asleep in her velvet-covered bed. He knelt beside her and kissed her hand. At last the evil spell was broken . . .

. . . And everyone woke up, just as the good fairy had planned!

The Prince and Princess fell in love and after a while they were married, and of course lived happily ever after.

To bed, to bed,
Says Sleepy-head;
Tarry a while, says Slow;
Put on the pan,
Says Greedy Nan,
We'll sup before we go.

See a pin and pick it up,
All the day you'll have good luck.
See a pin and let it lay,
Bad luck you'll have all the day.

Peter, Peter, pumpkin eater,
Had a wife and couldn't keep her;
He put her in a pumpkin shell,
And there he kept her very well.

If I had a donkey that wouldn't go,
Would I beat him? Oh no, no.
I'd put him in the barn and give him some corn.
The best little donkey that ever was born.

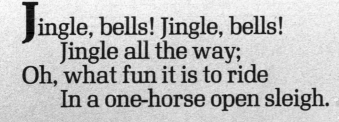

Jingle, bells! Jingle, bells!
  Jingle all the way;
Oh, what fun it is to ride
  In a one-horse open sleigh.

Hot cross buns! Hot cross buns!
One a penny, two a penny,
Hot cross buns!
If you have no daughters
Give them to your sons;
One a penny, two a penny
Hot cross buns.

To market, to market, to buy a fat pig,
Home again, home again, jiggety-jig;

MARKET

Pussy cat, pussy cat,
    Where have you been?
I've been to London
    To look at the Queen.

Pussy cat, pussy cat,
    What did you there?
I frightened a little mouse
    Under her chair.

To market, to market, to buy a fat hog,
Home again, home again, jiggety-jog.

Baa, baa, black sheep,
　　Have you any wool?
Yes, sir, yes, sir,
　　Three bags full;

One for the master,
　　And one for the dame,
And one for the little boy
　　Who lives down the lane.

Little Jack Horner
　　Sat in the corner,
Eating his Christmas pie;
　　He put in his thumb,
And pulled out a plum,
　　And said, What a good boy am I!

'Oranges and lemons,'
Say the bells of St Clement's.

'You owe me five farthings,'
Say the bells of St Martin's.

'When will you pay me?'
Say the bells of Old Bailey.

'When I grow rich,'
Say the bells of Shoreditch.

'When will that be?'
Say the bells of Stepney.

'I'm sure I don't know,'
Says the Great Bell of Bow.

Here comes the candle
To light you to bed,
Here comes the chopper,
To chop off your head.

One, two, three, four, five,
Once I caught a fish alive,
Six, seven, eight, nine, ten,
Then I let it go again.

Why did you let it go?
Because it bit my finger so.
Which finger did it bite?
This little finger on the right.

Three blind mice, see how they run!
They all ran after the farmer's wife,
Who cut off their tails with a carving knife,
Did you ever see such a thing in your life,
As three blind mice?

Mary had a little lamb,
  Its fleece was white as snow;
And everywhere that Mary went
  The lamb was sure to go.

It followed her to school one day,
  That was against the rule;
It made the children laugh and play
  To see a lamb at school.

SCHOOL

Cobbler, cobbler mend my shoe,
Get it done by half past two,
Stitch it up and stitch it down
And then I'll give you half a crown.

There was a little girl
Who had a little curl
Right in the middle of her forehead.

When she was good,
She was very, very good;
But when she was bad, she was horrid.

The Gingerbread Man

Once upon a time there lived an old woman, an old man and a little boy. Now one day the old woman was so busy in her kitchen she asked the little boy to help her. They were going to do some baking while the old man went into the garden to dig.

"Let's get started," said the old woman. "We have lots to do today." She told the little boy that if he worked hard, he could make something special.

The little boy found the rolling pin and baking tins. Next he got out the flour, the eggs and the butter. He weighed the sugar and beat the eggs. He even rolled out the pastry.

Very soon they had baked a big pile of cakes and pies. They made fancy little cakes with icing and sweets on top, and buns covered in chocolate and tarts filled with red jam. They looked delicious.

"We're almost done," said the old woman with a smile. "Have a look in my cookery book and find something special you would like to bake."

The little boy opened the book and found it at once. "I want to make the biggest Gingerbread Man in the world," he cried.

So the little boy found the largest baking tin that would fit into the oven. He cut out the Gingerbread Man shape then he gave him currants for eyes and buttons, and a slice of lemon peel for a mouth.

The old woman put the
Gingerbread Man into the
oven, and told the boy to keep
an eye on him, while she went
out into the garden.

It wasn't very long before he
heard strange noises coming
from the oven. First a tapping,
then a banging and then a very
loud knocking.

All at once, the oven door
burst open, and out jumped the
Gingerbread Man.

He dashed past the little boy
and straight out the kitchen
door. He ran outside, down the
path, and out of the garden
gate.

The old man, the old woman and the little boy
began to chase after him. But the Gingerbread Man
laughed and shouted, "Run! Run! As fast as you can!
You can't catch me, I'm the Gingerbread Man!"

"Free at last," he shouted, as he ran over hills and away. "No-one can catch me and eat me up — because I'm the Gingerbread Man."

On his way he passed some men resting under a tree. "Can't catch me," yelled the Gingerbread Man, as he sped by.

"It's too hot to run," shouted the men, "but if you come any closer, we'll eat you for our dinner."

But the Gingerbread Man just stuck out his tongue.

By now the Gingerbread
Man was beginning to enjoy his
freedom. He spied a big black
cat fast asleep in the sun. The
Gingerbread Man pulled her
whiskers as he ran by.

The cat sprang up and chased after the
Gingerbread Man trying to catch him with her sharp
claws. "Run! Run! As fast as you can! You can't
catch me, I'm the Gingerbread Man!"
The cat ran after the
Gingerbread Man for miles,
but she never caught him.

On and on he ran until he
heard a fierce dog barking in a
garden. "Can't catch me,"
teased the Gingerbread Man.
   The dog was so startled he
jumped over the gate and ran
after the Gingerbread Man. He
snapped and snarled at him,
and tried to bite him in half
with his sharp teeth.

"Run! Run! As fast as you can! You can't catch
me, I'm the Gingerbread Man!" The dog chased
after him until he was too tired to go any further. But
he never did catch the Gingerbread Man.

Next he passed a field of cows quietly munching the grass. The Gingerbread Man climbed up on the fence and shouted at the top of his voice. "Can't catch me, I'm the Gingerbread Man."

One of the cows lifted up her head, "I don't need to run after you," she mooed. "I can reach you from here." She was so big she almost swallowed the Gingerbread Man in one bite.

The Gingerbread Man fell off the fence in fright. He picked himself up and cried, "Run! Run! As fast as you can! You can't catch me, I'm the Gingerbread Man!" The cow went on quietly munching the grass.

The Gingerbread Man just kept on running until he came to a river. He sat down on the bank quite out of breath and feeling rather pleased with himself. "It must be true," he said out loud. "No-one can catch me. An old woman, an old man and a little boy can't catch me. The men resting under the tree couldn't either, nor could the black cat or the fierce dog, not even that silly cow."

The Gingerbread Man grinned. "I really am the most wonderful Gingerbread Man in the world."

Now hiding in the grass near the river bank was a Fox. He heard every word that the Gingerbread Man said and he licked his lips.

"Good day. What a fine
looking fellow you are," called
the Fox, as he strolled along the
river bank towards the
Gingerbread Man.
"Thank you, kind sir,"
smiled the Gingerbread Man.
"Run! Run! As fast as you can!

You can't catch me, I'm the Gingerbread Man!''

"I wouldn't dream of trying," said the Fox slyly. "Tell me, Gingerbread Man. How are you going to cross the river? Can you swim?"

The Gingerbread Man looked rather dismayed. "I can jump. I can do hand-stands. I can even balance on one leg. However, you are quite right, Mr. Fox, I cannot swim."

"Now I can swim very well," sniggered the Fox. "I have a wonderful idea, Gingerbread Man. If you

balance on my tail, I will take you across the river."
So the Fox and the Gingerbread Man started to
cross the water.

They hadn't gone very far before the Fox's tail
began to get wet. "Stand on my back," said the

Fox, "and you'll be alright."
So the Gingerbread man climbed onto his back.
Deeper and deeper they went. Soon the Fox's
back was under water. "Climb up onto my head,"
called the Fox, "or you'll get wet."

So the Gingerbread Man climbed onto his head.
A little further across the river the Fox's head
began to sink under the water. "Climb up on my
nose," shouted the Fox, "or you will drown."

The Gingerbread Man
climbed up onto the very top of
the Fox's nose.
    The Fox opened his mouth
wide and, SNAP, he gobbled
him up in one bite.

So that was the end of the poor Gingerbread Man.

"Run! Run! As fast as you can! You can't catch me, I'm the Gingerbread Man!"

And no-one ever did catch him . . . except the Fox.